W9-AFD-003

## Dear Parent:

Congratulations! Your child is taking the first steps on an exciting journey. The destination? Independent reading!

**STEP INTO READING®** will help your child get there. The program offers five steps to reading success. Each step includes fun stories and colorful art. There are also Step into Reading Sticker Books, Step into Reading Math Readers, Step into Reading Phonics Readers, Step into Reading Write-In Readers, and Step into Reading Phonics Boxed Sets—a complete literacy program with something for every child.

### Learning to Read, Step by Step!

Ready to Read **Preschool–Kindergarten**
**• big type and easy words • rhyme and rhythm • picture clues**
For children who know the alphabet and are eager to begin reading.

Reading with Help **Preschool–Grade 1**
**• basic vocabulary • short sentences • simple stories**
For children who recognize familiar words and sound out new words with help.

Reading on Your Own **Grades 1–3**
**• engaging characters • easy-to-follow plots • popular topics**
For children who are ready to read on their own.

Reading Paragraphs **Grades 2–3**
**• challenging vocabulary • short paragraphs • exciting stories**
For newly independent readers who read simple sentences with confidence.

Ready for Chapters **Grades 2–4**
**• chapters • longer paragraphs • full-color art**
For children who want to take the plunge into chapter books but still like colorful pictures.

**STEP INTO READING®** is designed to give every child a successful reading experience. The grade levels are only guides. Children can progress through the steps at their own speed, developing confidence in their reading, no matter what their grade.

Remember, a lifetime love of reading starts with a single step!

Visit us on the Web!
StepIntoReading.com
randomhouse.com/kids

Educators and librarians, for a variety of teaching tools, visit us at RHTeachersLibrarians.com

ISBN: 978-0-449-81387-4 (trade) – ISBN: 978-0-375-97155-6 (lib. bdg.)

Printed in the United States of America 10 9 8 7 6 5 4 3 2 1

STEP INTO READING® STEP 2

# SUPER SOAP

Based on the teleplay "Super Soap"
by Clark Stubbs

Illustrated by Lorraine O'Connell

Random House New York

Milli, Geo, and Bot

are heroes.

They are
Team Umizoomi.
They live in Umi City.

Silly Bear is
Team Umizoomi's friend.
Uh-oh! He spilled glue.
The toy duck is stuck
on Silly Bear!

Team Umizoomi
must help Silly Bear.

"Super Soap will get Silly Bear clean," says Geo.

"Silly Bear's cave is
in the Umi City Forest,"
says Bot.

“It’s time for action!”
says Team Umizoomi.
They run to help
Silly Bear.

Team Umizoomi stops
at a big gate.
It is locked.

DoorMouse has the key.

He is asleep.

"A drum will wake up DoorMouse," says Geo.

Geo uses
his Super Shapes.
He makes the drum.

Bang! Bang! Bang!

The drum is loud.

DoorMouse wakes up.
He unlocks the big gate.

Team Umizoomi runs into the Umi City Forest.

Team Umizoomi stops at the river.

"Can we hop across on the rocks?" asks Bot.

Milli knows which rocks are safe.

She uses Pattern Power.

The pattern is
orange rock,
purple rock, green rock.

Orange rock.

Purple rock. Green rock.

Team Umizoomi hops

across the river.

Team Umizoomi is
at Silly Bear's cave!

Team Umizoomi
washes Silly Bear
with Super Soap.
Now the toy duck
is not stuck.

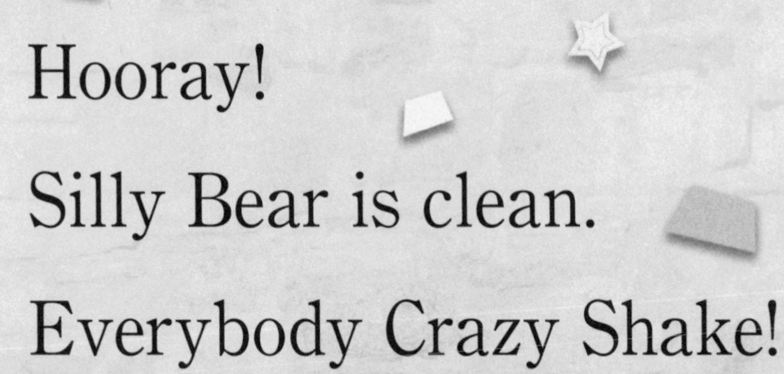

Hooray!

Silly Bear is clean.

Everybody Crazy Shake!

DATE DUE
FEB 13